We enjoy life most of all
when we are working or playing hard.

Our bodies are designed
to put back what we take out.
Food provides energy.
Sleep and rest allow
our bodies and minds to recover.

Sometimes, though, things get out of hand.
Our bodies and minds can be overstretched.

Illness, injury,
lack of food or sleep,
emotional upsets or worry,
all cause stress.

This book helps us to recognize the signs
and to learn how to deal with them.

Relax

by Catherine O'Neill
Illustrated by Toni Goffe

Child's Play (International) Ltd

Swindon   Auburn ME   Sydney

© M. Twinn 1993   ISBN 978-0-85953-790-2   Printed in China

This impression 2008   www.childs-play.com

Library of Congress Number 93-29059

A catalogue reference for this book is available from the British Library

Life has its UPs
. . . and DOWNs.

We can cope with them
most of the time.

Pain and stress
can be useful warning signals and
are a necessary part of our lives.

Once the causes are removed,
we recover quickly.

We may even laugh about them.

What is tension? What makes it happen?

Everybody is different.

What we find funny,
others may find scary.

Don't be ashamed of your feelings.

Don't hide them away
– especially from yourself.

Sometimes, friends hurt us.

They leave us out of things,
make fun of us or bully us.
We feel let down.

Sad things, like someone dying,
can make us tense.

It is horrible
when your cat or your dog
or your pet goldfish dies.

It is a very mixed-up feeling
of being angry, sad, lost and very tense.

Don't hide these feelings away.
There is nothing to be ashamed of.

A new baby at home may make you feel a bit jealous, or worry about being pushed out.

If the baby wants attention, all it has to do is cry.
It's enough to give us a headache!

Remember,
you were a baby once.

Your parents haven't
stopped loving you.

You are still their baby!

What's happening here?

Family arguments are upsetting,
even when we are not involved.

When we are angry, we say terrible things.
We may even want to break something or hit someone.

What are these parents arguing about?

Parents can be very difficult.

Sometimes, they make us feel it is our fault.

What do you think this argument is about?
Yes, money!

Money doesn't grow on trees.
Money can cause worries in most families.

Especially, when parents are out of work.

Sometimes, we feel tense and don't know why.
It's as though we are picking up signals on special antennae.

Listen to these signals. They seldom let you down.

Sometimes, we feel threatened.

Sometimes, we don't like someone, and we can't say why.
Is it the way they look at us or the way they talk?
Maybe, they ask us to do something that makes us feel uneasy?

Has this ever happened to you?

We may feel tense
when we are made to do things we don't want to do:

> like eating food we don't enjoy;
> or reading aloud in class;
> or exams;
> or playing games we don't like.

We may be afraid that we are not good enough or look silly.

Time is a big worry. Thinking about the past.
Being anxious about the future.

Having to be somewhere on time.
Having to catch a bus or a train.

Perhaps it will be late.
Perhaps it will be full.
Perhaps it won't stop.
Perhaps someone will
push in and take our place.

Maybe, we are afraid
we will get into trouble
or let someone down.

We spend a lot of time
worrying about things
that don't happen!

Fear comes in all shapes and sizes.

Some people are afraid of the dark.

Others are frightened by spiders
or things that creep and crawl.

Strange noises or ghost stories may fill you with fear.

Some people are frightened of tests or exams.
Just thinking about them makes them feel ill.

Fear can give you a horrible feeling in your stomach.

How can we recognize stress?

Some of the signs or signals our body gives us, are when . . .

. . . we sweat

. . . we blush

. . . we shake

Our breathing gets faster. Sometimes, it stops.
We may even faint.

We feel we just have to get away . . .

We clench our fists and jaw. . .	We bite our lips, grind our teeth. . .	Our heart beats faster . . .

Sometimes, being tense stops you thinking properly.
Your mind goes into a spin. You can't get the words out.
You stammer. You can't understand what people are saying.
Or, maybe, you just can't stop talking. On and on and on!

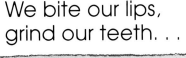

HURRY UP, WE HAVEN'T GOT ALL DAY!

We feel as though we are wound up like an elastic band, tighter and tighter, until we are ready to snap.

At night, we can't get to sleep. We have scary dreams.
Our fears creep out of the surface of our mind.
We wake in panic or wet the bed.

These things happen to everyone at one time or another.
Yet they make us feel embarrassed and guilty.
We don't want anyone to find out.

What does 'relax' mean?

Relaxing is that lovely feeling when you just let go,
like at bathtime, or when you are swinging in a hammock.

Try and relax your body now.
Let yourself go all floppy.

There! That feels better!

Now relax your mind.

Cuddle up with your Teddy.
He will never let you down.

What can you do to make yourself feel better?

Sometimes, we can't make the things
that make us tense go away.
So, we have to find ways of coping.

Learning to explore or understand a problem
will make us strong. This is better than running away from it.

Reading this book is a good start.
If you can share it with a brother or sister
or a friend, that is even better.
Talking to people we trust is a great help, too.

Which side of bed did we get out of this morning?
Attitudes and moods are like choosing what to wear.

Which mood shall I put on?

Let's learn to be comfortable with ourselves.

Try to see yourself in a good light
and be positive about what you want to achieve.

You don't have to be Number One
in order to feel good about yourself.

SMILEY HAPPY THOUGHT SAD CRYING ANGRY
                -FUL

Think about your friends.
What a mixture of shapes, sizes and minds!

They are all different, aren't they?
But it doesn't matter, does it?

One of the first things we must do in order to relax is accept ourselves. Being honest with ourselves makes us stronger and makes it harder for unkind people to hurt us.

Tense-Stretch-Relax Games

When our minds are tense, our bodies are tense, too.
Relaxing your body will help you relax your mind.

Shall we learn some games which will help?

Hands

Squeeze each of your hands into a tight ball.
Pretend you are clutching something precious.
Squeeze really tight.

Now, stretch open your hands. Spread your fingers.
Make your fingers grow, grow, grow.

Now, drop your hands. Let them go. They are SO heavy.

As you play, can you see a picture in your mind?

Your tight fist has become a flower bud,
opening slowly in the sunshine.
The petals stretch out in the warm sun.
Now the flower closes again.

Feet, Legs, Bottom, Tummy, Arms

Lie down.

Is there someone who will help?
A parent, a brother or a sister? Or a friend?
Get them to wrap you in a cosy blanket.
Maybe, they will talk gently and help you relax
each part of your body.

Think of your feet – they are relaxed and heavy.
They are so heavy, you just can't lift them.
Imagine them in a bowl of warm water.
Now, this lovely, warm feeling is going up your legs
and slowly filling your body.
Now, let your hands feel tingly, then your arms . . .
You can gradually go all the way round your body.

Massage can help you relax, too.

Day Dreams

Once your body is relaxed, think of something
which makes you feel happy or of someone you really like.

Imagine running through long grass or cuddling a rabbit.
Think what fur or velvet feels like.

Can you hear the sound of the sea or birds singing?

Think of the colour, fragrance and feel of a rose petal.

Or remember a time at school when you have done well.
Think about good times with friends.

Imagine anything you like –
whatever makes you feel happy and relaxed.

Breathing

When we breathe, we take in the air which our body needs.
Air gives us the energy to run, talk and sleep
and do all the things we want to do.

It is like filling a car up to keep it running.
When we are tense, we may not breathe properly.
This stops our body from working well.

Here are some games to help your breathing.

Put your hands on your chest just above your tummy.
Breathe in slowly through your nose.
Then out slowly through your nose or mouth.

Can you feel your ribs and your tummy move out
when you breathe in and move in when you breathe out?

Imagine that inside your chest is a big, yellow balloon.
As you breathe in, imagine this balloon slowly filling up.
As you slowly breathe out, let the yellow balloon become
smaller and smaller and smaller.

ha ha ha HAAAAH

Pretend you are a dog. You are puffed out.
Take a deep breath. Breathe out.
Make three short panting sounds: "ha, ha, ha".
Then a long, tired "HAAAAH".
Try this several times.

Now, imagine you are a laughing mouse.
Breathe in, and as you breathe out,
in short bursts, say, "Hee, hee, hee, hee".

Make your tummy move in with each "hee".

hee hee hee hee hee hee hee

Now, you can play the 'buzzing game'.
Pretend you are a bee buzzing around a flower.
Make a long buzzing sound on one breath: "zzzzzzz".
Zzzzzz is a lovely sound to make.
This humming sound helps you calm down and ignore
all the hustle and bustle going on around you.

Now, pretend you are a little plane.
Make the noise of the engine.
Make your voice rise as you go up into the sky.
Make your voice fall as you come into land.

Now, you are a big tree, growing tall.
As you breathe in, move your branches
in a big circle, up and round.
Breathe out, as you bring them down to your side.

Imagine you are the wind.
Breathe out: blow the sea onto the land.
Breathe in: suck the sea back again.
Now, blow it out again.
Keep the sea moving, as you breathe in and out.

Relaxing Games for Shoulders, Back and Neck.

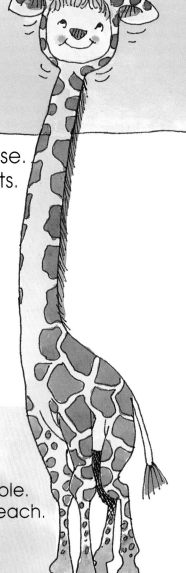

Different parts of our body can become tense.
Shoulders, backs and necks are danger spots.

Shoulders and Neck

Pretend you are a monkey.
1. Move your shoulders as high as you can, up to your ears, and breathe in.
2. As you breathe out, drop your shoulders and dangle your arms by your side.

   Repeat this slowly, several times.

Now, stretch up your neck.
Make it feel long like a swan's or a giraffe's.
1. Pull your shoulders down as far as you can.
2. Stretch out your neck. Make it as long as possible.
3. Stretch a bit more for a tender leaf just out of reach. Got it! Let go and relax.

   Repeat, several times.

Shoulders and Neck

You are a weary robot or a wise old owl.

Try rolling your head.
1. Tip your head forward, so your chin nearly touches your chest.
2. Slowly turn to your right shoulder.
3. Straighten your head.
4. Then turn to your left shoulder.
5. Bring your head forward and repeat in the opposite direction.
6. Then just let your head go floppy.

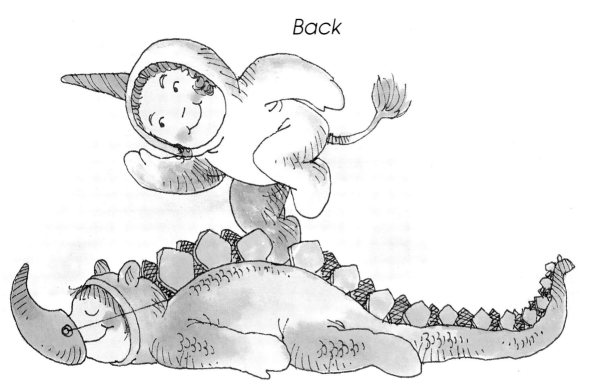

Where is your backbone (or spine)? Run your fingers down it.
Can you feel all those little bones in a long line?
They stretch from your neck all the way down to your bottom.

Imagine you are a dinosaur. A friendly unicorn
is tip-toeing up and down your spine, bone by bone.

Pretend you are a friendly cat who loves being stroked.
Imagine someone is stroking you from your neck down
along your spine, very slowly, soothing away horrible feelings,
getting rid of all the tension which has been stored up.

Imagine this tension as dirty grey lumps being gently and
carefully stroked away.

Head and Face

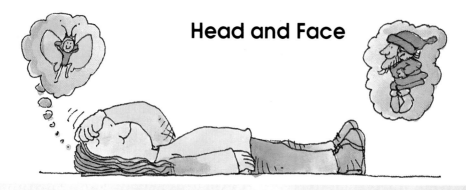

Put your hands on your face.
Tickle very gently with your finger tips.

Close your eyes. Your fingers are tiny fairies dancing lightly over your eyelids, over your cheeks and up to your ears.

Your fingers change into hobgoblins.
The hobgoblins dance heavily, round and round.

There are hundreds of muscles in your face. Feel them relax.

Keep your eyes closed. Look towards your tummy.
Think about a lovely deep blue colour.

Do you have worry lines on your forehead?
Imagine your friend the unicorn dragging a soft blanket over them, smoothing them away.

Do you like animals? Pretend to be your favourite animal.
Make the animal lick its lips, swallow, hum.
Yawn a big yawn. Stretch its mouth wide open.

Make a happy face. Make a big smile.
Make a surprised face. Raise your eyebrows as high as you can.

Really make your animal's mouth move
and say "ee, oo, ee, oo, eeeee."

Stretch your lips for "eeeee." Then make them round for "ooooo."
Then just let your animal relax.
Imagine someone stroking your animal's head.

Lucky Me!

Sometimes, how we see ourselves is very different from how we really are. When we are tense, we may feel small and sad. Why don't you draw the way you are feeling?

Breathe in some lovely deep breaths.
As you breathe out, get rid of all the bad images you have.
Breathe out all your worries, all the things
you don't like about yourself. Watch them drift away.

Stand up and stretch. Imagine yourself taller and in control.
Smile and feel happy about yourself.
Now, breathe in slowly.
Breathe in all the good things about yourself.
There is plenty to smile about. Breathe out and relax.

Now, imagine you are a tense spring or a wobbly, shaky puppet.
Breathe in and say "ha" as you breathe out.

The tense spring has turned into a happy, floppy rag doll.

Life has its ups and its downs.

Everyone gets tense.

Things happen to make some people more tense than others

Some people can relax more easily than others.

The secret key is keeping your balance between tension and relaxation, sadness and happiness.

When we live in harmony with ourselves and others,
life is good.

Remember, everyone has fears and anxieties.
It can be horrible. But it is normal, too!

THE CHILD'S POSE

Let us finish with a lovely exercise to help you to enjoy silence and calm. It is called the 'Child's Pose'.

Kneel down. Sit on your heels.
Put your head on the ground and
rest your arms at your sides.
Enjoy a few moments of rest
away from all the noise around you.